W9-ATY-633

Cinderella
and the
Beanstalk

Crabtree Publishing Company

www.crabtreebooks.com
1-800-387-7650

PMB 59051,
350 Fifth Ave., 59th Floor
New York, NY 10118

616 Welland Ave.
St. Catharines, ON
L2M 5V6

Published by Crabtree Publishing in 2013

Series editor: Louise John
Series Design: Emil Dacanay
Design: Lisa Peacock
Consultant: Shirley Bickler
Editor: Kathy Middleton
Proofreaders: Kelly McNiven, Crystal Sikkens
Notes to adults: Reagan Miller
Print and production coordinator: Katherine Berti

Text © Hilary Robinson 2013
Illustration © Simona Sanfilippo 2013

Printed in the U.S.A./072014/SN20140630

First published in
2013 by Wayland
(A division of Hachette
Children's Books)

**Library and Archives Canada
Cataloguing in Publication**

Robinson, Hilary, 1962-
    Cinderella and the beanstalk / written by
Hilary Robinson ; illustrated by Simona Sanfilippo.

(Tadpoles: fairytale jumbles)
Issued also in electronic format.
ISBN 978-0-7787-1156-8 (bound).
--ISBN 978-0-7787-1161-2 (pbk.)

    I. Sanfilippo, Simona II. Title. III. Series:
Tadpoles (St. Catharines, Ont.). Fairytale jumbles

PZ7.R6235Ci 2013   j823'.914   C2012-908175-2

**Library of Congress
Cataloging-in-Publication Data**

Robinson, Hilary, 1962-
 Cinderella and the beanstalk / written by Hilary
Robinson ; illustrated by Simona Sanfilippo.
    pages cm. -- (Tadpoles: fairytale jumbles)
    Summary: "Jack and Cinderella climb the beanstalk
and find a giant fairy godmother. Can she help
them get to the prince's ball?"-- Provided by
publisher.
    ISBN 978-0-7787-1156-8 (reinforced library binding
: alk. paper) -- ISBN 978-0-7787-1161-2 (pbk. : alk.
paper) -- ISBN 978-1-4271-9304-9 (electronic pdf) --
ISBN 978-1-4271-9228-8 (electronic html)
    [1. Stories in rhyme. 2. Characters in literature--
Fiction. 3. Magic--Fiction.] I. Sanfilippo, Simona,
illustrator. II. Title.

    PZ8.3.R575Ci 2013
    [E]--dc23
                                        2012047921

C.I

Cinderella and the Beanstalk

Written by Hilary Robinson
Illustrated by Simona Sanfilippo

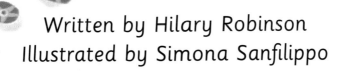

Crabtree Publishing Company
www.crabtreebooks.com

"Jack! Jack! You lazy boy!
We have no food to eat.
Take our cow to market
and sell her for some meat."

"And Cinderella, get to work!
Our dresses are too tight.

Mend them! Wash them! Press them!
It's the prince's ball tonight!"

"Is your cow for sale, my boy?
She's the finest I have seen.

I don't have any money,
but I'll swap her for this bean."

"This magic bean," the old man said,
"will grow and change your life.

If you plant it in your garden,
it will help the prince find a wife!"

The sisters flew into a rage
and threw the bean outside.

Jack ran into the kitchen
to find a place to hide.

Cinderella shouted, "Jack! Look up!
The beanstalk has grown high.

Let's go and climb it right away
and see what's in the sky!"

At the very top they heard a voice that sang out, "Fee, Fi, Fo!"

A giant godmother waved her wand.
"Off to the ball you go!"

A cloud became a carriage,
and stars her dress and shawl.

Jack sat up in the driver's seat
and took them to the ball.

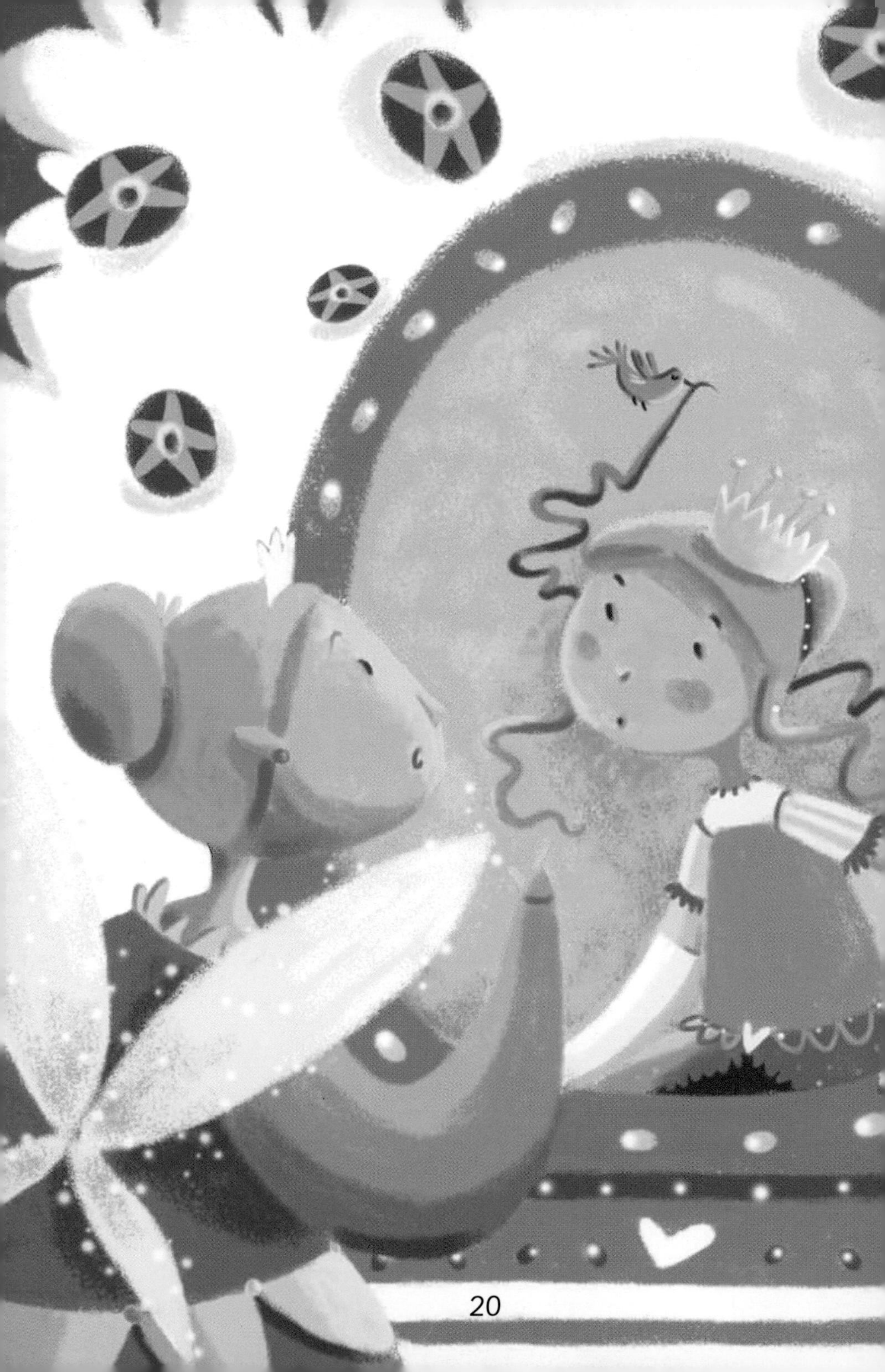

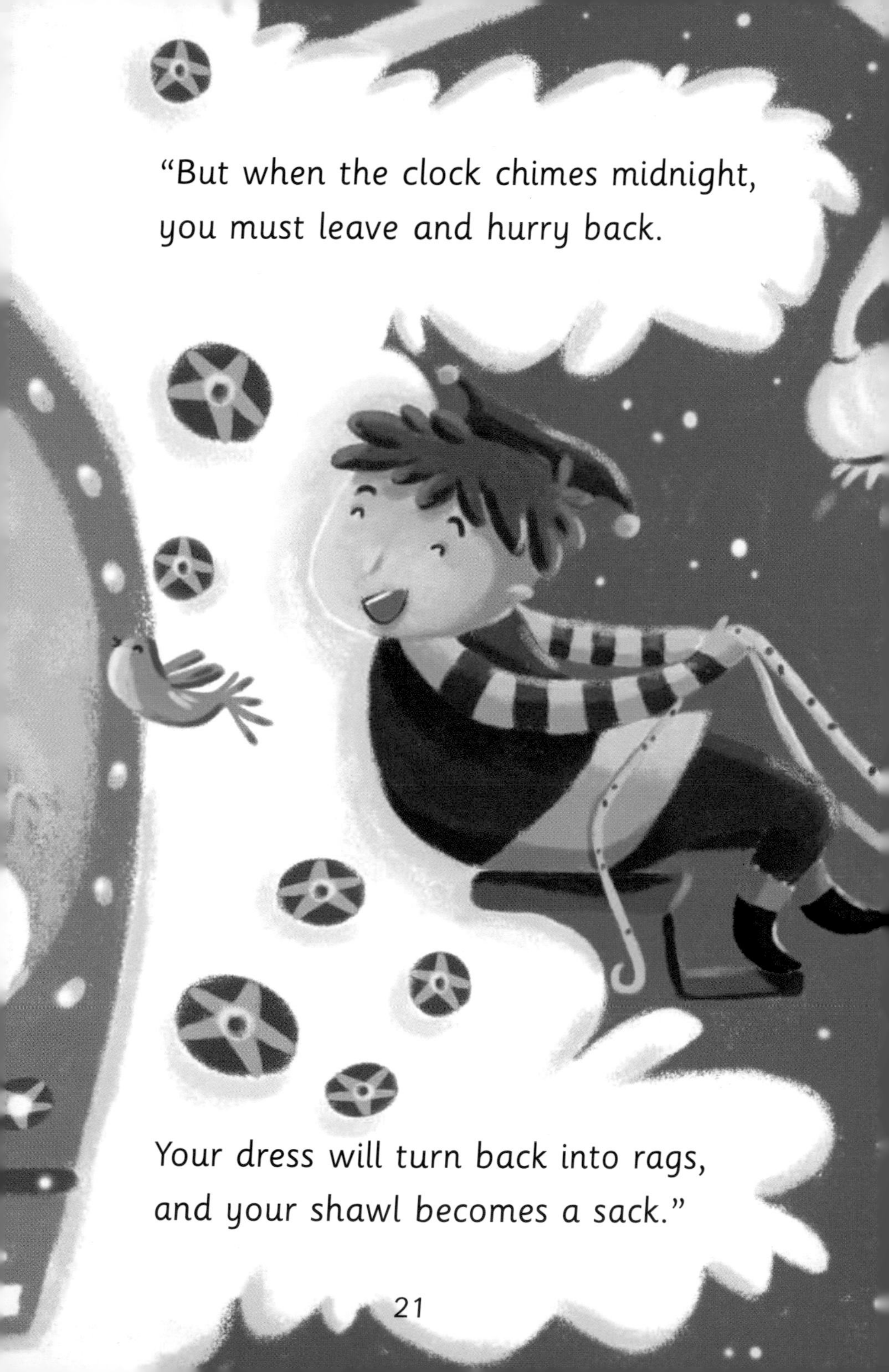

“But when the clock chimes midnight,
you must leave and hurry back.

Your dress will turn back into rags,
and your shawl becomes a sack.”

The prince saw Cinderella
and danced with her all night.

But when the clock struck midnight,
she disappeared from sight.

He found the shoe she'd left behind
and set off on a ride!

"I'll find the owner of this shoe,
and she shall be my bride!"

The ugly sisters tried to squeeze
their feet into the shoe.

The prince saw Cinderella and said,
"This shoe belongs to you!"

The ugly sisters went out to climb
the beanstalk, but they found

that when they got just halfway up...
it toppled to the ground!

The prince and Cinderella
were married the next day.

Jack became the palace chef,
and the others ran away!

Notes for Adults

Tadpoles: Fairytale Jumbles are designed for transitional and early fluent readers. The books may also be used for a read-aloud or shared reading with younger children. **Tadpoles: Fairytale Jumbles** are humorous stories with a unique twist on traditional fairytales. Each story can be compared to the original fairytale, or appreciated on its own. Fairytales are a key type of literary text found in the Common Core State Standards.

THE FOLLOWING BEFORE, DURING, AND AFTER READING ACTIVITY SUGGESTIONS SUPPORT LITERACY SKILL DEVELOPMENT AND CAN ENRICH SHARED READING EXPERIENCES:

1. Make reading fun! Choose a time to read when you and the child are relaxed and have time to share the story.
2. Before reading, invite the child to preview the book. The child can read the title, look at the illustrations, skim through the text, and make predictions as to what will happen in the story. Predicting sets a clear purpose for reading and learning.
3. During reading, encourage the child to monitor his or her understanding by asking questions to draw conclusions, making connections, and using context clues to understand unfamiliar words.
4. After reading, ask the child to review his or her predictions. Were they correct? Discuss different parts of the story, including main characters, setting, main events, and the problem and solution. If the child is familiar with the original fairytale, invite he or she to identify the similarities and differences between the two versions of the story.
5. Encourage the child to use his or her imagination to create fairytale jumbles based on other familiar stories.
6. Give praise! Children learn best in a positive environment.

IF YOU ENJOYED THIS BOOK, WHY NOT TRY ANOTHER TADPOLES: FAIRYTALE JUMBLES STORY?

Goldilocks and the Wolf	*978-0-7787-8023-6 RLB* *978-1-4271-9156-4 Ebook (HTML)*	*978-0-7787-8034-2 PB* *978-1-4271-9148-9 Ebook (PDF)*
Snow White and the Enormous Turnip	*978-0-7787-8024-3 RLB* *978-1-4271-9158-8 Ebook (HTML)*	*978-0-7787-8035-9 PB* *978-1-4271-9150-2 Ebook (PDF)*
The Elves and the Emperor	*978-0-7787-8025-0 RLB* *978-1-4271-9159-5 Ebook (HTML)*	*978-0-7787-8036-6 PB* *978-1-4271-9151-9 Ebook (PDF)*
Three Pigs and a Gingerbread Man	*978-0-7787-8026-7 RLB* *978-1-4271-9157-1 Ebook (HTML)*	*978-0-7787-8037-3 PB* *978-1-4271-9149-6 Ebook (PDF)*
Rapunzel and the Billy Goats	*978-0-7787-1154-4 RLB* *978-1-4271-9226-4 Ebook (HTML)*	*978-0-7787-1158-2 PB* *978-1-4271-9302-5 Ebook (PDF)*
Beauty and the Pea	*978-0-7787-1155-1 RLB* *978-1-4271-9227-1 Ebook (HTML)*	*978-0-7787-1159-9 PB* *978-1-4271-9303-2 Ebook (PDF)*
Hansel, Gretel, and the Ugly Duckling	*978-0-7787-1157-5 RLB* *978-1-4271-9229-5 Ebook (HTML)*	*978-0-7787-1166-7 PB* *978-1-4271-9305-6 Ebook (PDF)*

VISIT WWW.CRABTREEBOOKS.COM FOR OTHER CRABTREE BOOKS.